Robin Alexis

Donkeys,
Humans,
Butterflies,
and
Guns

Donkeys, Humans, Butterflies, and Guns

Published in the United States of America
First Publication: May 2023
(Divine Communications)
Donkeys, Humans, Butterflies, and Guns ISBN: 979-8-9881534-0-5
(paperback)

For more information about other publications by this author, please visit: www.RobinAlexis.com

Preface

Donkeys, Humans, Butterflies, and Guns is a parable about a donkey and a family of butterflies, and how they see the human dilemma concerning guns.

Albert Einstein famously said, "*If you can't explain it to a six year old, then you don't understand it yourself.*" Mister Rogers knew this. He explained everything in terms that a six-year-old could understand.

Mister Rogers asked, "*What do you do with the mad that you feel when you feel so mad you could bite?*" He would tell us to stop stop stop, when we're angry, to breathe, and think, and choose to do something that won't hurt anyone else. In other words, even if you've always been more like a stubborn donkey, you can choose to transform and behave like a gentle butterfly.

May this story about how animals see each other, and how they see us, help us all to become better humans.

Donkeys, Humans, Butterflies, and Guns – Robin Alexis

This book is dedicated to responsible gun owners everywhere.

DONKEYS, HUMANS, BUTTERFLIES, AND GUNS

Billie the Butterfly had a special affection for Donna the Donkey. Billie knew that as a butterfly he would have only up to 30 days maximum to live. He was going to make sure that Donna knew how much he loved her before his butterfly days were over! He spent much of his time perched on her ear whispering words like:

"We may be very different from one another, but you are my love and I'll never leave you."

One hot autumn day Donna was in an apple orchard, working with a human. Billie was keeping her company, whispering in her ear as she worked. The human paid no attention to Billie, or to Donna, either. Donna tripped over an apple on the ground and fell, and all the apples in the baskets she was carrying on her back tumbled out of the baskets, rolling everywhere!

The human got very angry, cursing in multiple languages! The human didn't help Donna get back on her feet. He didn't pick up the apples and put them back in the baskets. The human didn't ask anyone else to help! He just got mad, and then he started kicking Donna!!

Donna the Donkey lay on the ground, unable to move. Every time the human's steel-toed boots struck her belly, she groaned in pain!

Donna came to her senses. She had to get the human to stop kicking her!

"Golly!" she muttered to herself, "Maybe I was a little bit distracted, but it feels like he's trying to kill me!"

Still, all this thinking did nothing to get Donna back up on her hooves. She was stuck.

Donna the Donkey must have been psychic. A moment later, the human screamed in more horrible foul language, "I am going to kill you for ruining my apple picking day!" The human pulled out a concealed gun and aimed it at Donna the Donkey.

As he took aim at Donna, the human tripped on some apples, just as Donna had done earlier, but even that didn't give the human pause! Oh, no! He ignored his own misstep, but became even angrier at Donna.

In desperation, using his butterfly superpowers, Billie, who had been watching in horror, summoned his butterfly friends to fly around the human to confuse him. They were hoping for a miracle, even though they knew it was a long shot. As they flew to the rescue, they all fluttered as loudly as they could, saying, "It is not okay to kill the donkey!"

But the human wasn't listening.

The butterflies knew they had to do something NOW. Billie, along with hundreds of Billie's butterfly friends, attacked, madly fluttering their wings. They all landed on the human's hands! They were trying to stop his finger from firing the gun!

Their plan didn't work. The human pulled the trigger.

Billie and all the other butterflies tried to create a barrier to protect Donna from the human's bullets. But butterflies are no match for even one bullet, and certainly not for many bullets. It was a bloody massacre. A donkey, many butterflies, and many apples were blown to smithereens. When he was done shooting, the human was covered with blood, butterfly guts, and applesauce.

After the human fired the gun, all the other humans who were working in the apple orchard left their own donkeys and came running. They yelled,

One small human looking aghast at the heap of dead butterflies on top of a dead donkey surrounded by smooshed apples innocently asked, "What will happen to the gun that did this?"

The child's parent replied, "It's not the gun's fault." The child blinked once, then asked, "Then why are you all yelling about banning guns?"

While the humans were yelling about banning guns, Donna and Billie and all the other butterflies' souls floated up to heaven. They looked down on the chaos below. Even though they knew none of this was their fault, they were still distressed that they had been unable to stop the human from using his gun to express his anger.

What happened to the murderous human? Well, the police came and the human who shot the gun got arrested for bringing a loaded weapon into a public apple orchard, for potentially endangering other humans, and for destroying the orchard owner's property. He was led away in handcuffs. On the evening news, the news anchor announced that the human had been released from jail on $500 bail. They gave his gun back to him and sent him home.

Donna the Donkey, Billie the Butterfly, and all of Billie's friends looked at the humans below with sadness. The entire situation was just simply overkill. They were glad to be away from the insanity.

Billie and Donna looked at each other, shocked and suddenly delightfully aware that once their souls had left their bodies, they were together in the heavenly realms!

SURPRISE!!!

It had never mattered that one of them was a butterfly and one was a donkey! Love Transcends Death!!! Love transcends physical differences! No human, no guns, can stop the pure and eternal power of love!!! Their beloved butterfly friends were with them in heaven, too! *Woo Hoo!!!*

Donna and the butterflies had a meeting in heaven. Donna said, "Maybe when humans feel themselves getting mad, they could just pause for a moment and take a deep breath. They could hold their breath for a few seconds and then exhale slowly, and maybe put a hand over their heart and thank it for beating."

Donkeys, Humans, Butterflies, and Guns – Robin Alexis

17

Billie the Butterfly snarked, "Maybe humans need to have their hearts examined, along with their heads, before they are allowed to bear arms."

The butterflies all waved their butterfly wings in enthusiastic agreement. One butterfly asked, "How can we tell them that? Humans don't understand us, remember? We all got shot to death!"

Billie the Butterfly suggested, "Maybe we could make a cloud that forms the right words in every human language?"

The other butterflies all thought it was worth a try, and Donna the Donkey agreed. The butterflies created beautiful message clouds all around the world, telling people to examine their hearts and their heads, but no humans have looked up yet.

Donna the Donkey, Billie the Butterfly, and all of his butterfly friends are still waiting for at least one human to look up and see their message.

Will you be the first one to look up at the clouds? Will you let love lead to the solutions?

A portion of the proceeds from sales of this story will be directed to **beewellhive.org**.

Donkeys, Humans, Butterflies, and Guns – Robin Alexis

23

Elizabeth Diane and Robin Alexis, who created this book, are creating their next book about bees. Please donate to Bee Well Hive NFP (not for profit 501,c,3) to support the publication of their book. Because bees are better than bullets at making people happy 😃

Please visit Bee Well Hive NFP's website:

beewellhive.org

Donkeys, Humans, Butterflies, and Guns – Robin Alexis

Publications by Robin Alexis

<u>Available now:</u>

Spirit Lady: The Gift of Robin's Song
Ebook, paperback, hardcover, and audiobook

Raising Humanity: Why We All Must Remember
Ebook, paperback, and hardcover

Donkeys, Humans, Butterflies, and Guns
Ebook, paperback

<u>Future Releases:</u>

Raising Humanity: Why We All Must Remember
Audiobook

Love Letters from Heaven: Three Peas in a Pod
Ebook, paperback

If you enjoyed reading *Donkeys, Humans, Butterflies, and Guns*, please leave a positive review with the retailer of your choice. Thank you.

Best Selling Amazon Author Robin Alexis is available for 1-on-1 phone readings and personalized Reiki Healing Weeks. Join her on-line community "The Soul Spa" at **robinalexis.com**